Clifford
and the
Halloween
Parade

Library of Congress Cataloging-in-Publication Data is available.

ISBN-13: 978-0-439-09834-2
ISBN-10: 0-439-09834-3

15 14 13   18 19/0

Printed in the U.S.A. 40 • This edition first printing, August 2008

NORMAN BRIDWELL

Clifford
and the
Halloween Parade

SCHOLASTIC INC.

Clifford sees a bat.

Clifford sees a cat.

Clifford sees a rat.

It is Halloween!
What will Clifford be?

A boy brings a ladder.

A girl brings a hose.

The boy brings a light that flashes.

Here comes the boy in a raincoat, hat, and boots.

Here comes the girl in a
raincoat, hat, and boots.

They climb on Clifford.

Clifford is a fire engine.
The boy and girl are firefighters.

The Halloween parade will soon begin.

The boy, the girl, and Clifford come first.
Then come the bat, the cat, and the rat.

Happy Halloween, everybody!

• Word List •

a	hat
and	here
are	hose
bat	in
be	is
begin	it
boots	ladder
boy	light
brings	on
cat	parade
Clifford	raincoat
climb	rat
comes	sees
engine	soon
everybody	that
fire	the
firefighters	then
first	they
flashes	today
girl	what
Halloween	will
happy	